To Tim
From DAD

BUNNICULA
strikes again!

JAMES HOWE

illustrations by Alan Daniel

BUNNICULA
strikes again!

Aladdin Paperbacks

New York London Toronto Sydney Singapore

First Aladdin Paperbacks edition June 2001

Text copyright © 1999 by James Howe
Illustrations copyright © 1999 by Alan Daniel

Aladdin Paperbacks
An imprint of Simon & Schuster
Children's Publishing Division
1230 Avenue of the Americas
New York, NY 10020

Also available in an Atheneum Books for Young Readers hardcover edition
Designed by Ann Bobco
The text for this book was set in Berkeley.
The illustrations were rendered in pencil.

Manufactured in the United States of America

20 19 18 17 16 15 14 13

The Library of Congress has cataloged the hardcover edition as follows:
Howe, James.
Bunnicula strikes again! / by James Howe.
p.   cm.
Summary: When Bunnicula the rabbit starts acting strangely, the Monroe dogs and cat renew their suspicions that he is a vampire.
ISBN-13: 978-0-689-81463-1 (hc.)   ISBN-10: 0-689-81463-1 (hc.)
[1. Dogs—Fiction. 2. Cats—Fiction. 3. Rabbits—Fiction. 4. Vampires—Fiction.]
I. Title
PZ7.H83727But   1999
[Fic]—dc21
99-20419
ISBN-13: 978-0-689-81462-4 (Aladdin pbk.)
ISBN-10: 0-689-81462-3 (Aladdin pbk.)

Contents

To Harold's Editors Extraordinaire—
Jonathan J. Lanman
and
Jean Karl

[EDITOR'S NOTE]

LOOKING back on my years as an editor of fine literature, I can name many honors and associations of which I am proud. Yet one stands out as the apex of my career—the unique privilege of having edited the work of Harold, canine author extraordinaire. How many in my position have received a manuscript from the clenched jaws of its creator? Who else has known the pleasure of reading a novelist's new work for the very first time while the novelist himself lies at one's feet, snoring contentedly? What publishing professional has successfully entertained an out-of-town author with a handful of doggie biscuits and a bowl of cocoa? Other editors may dream of such things, but I have known them!

And yet, numerous books and countless doggie biscuits later, the unanswered questions remain: Where did Harold learn to type and how does he manage it with those big paws of his? What does he do with the early drafts of his work—bury them in the backyard? Doesn't anybody notice all that missing typing paper? If a tree falls in a forest and there is no one around to hear it, does it still make a sound?

Alas, these questions are destined to remain unanswered—small mysteries within the greater mystery of life itself. For although Harold is able to communicate via the written word—and, in ways that are incomprehensible to mere humans such as you and I, to speak to his fellow animals—he remains mute (other than the occasional "woof") in face-to-face contact. As delighted as I am to see him when he drops by my office, I don't count on much in the way of scintillating conversation.

Thus it was that when he last appeared at my door with a manuscript gripped between his teeth, I invited him in, proffered the usual cocoa and dog biscuits, and—without a word exchanged between us—proceeded to read his latest book as he curled up at my feet and went to sleep. First, I read the note that accompanied the manuscript, which read:

My dearest friend and esteemed colleague,

We have come a long way together since my first book, Bunnicula: A Rabbit-Tale of Mystery. *Little did we know that my life, which until Bunnicula's arrival had been decidedly unremarkable, would thereafter be filled with ad-*

ventures and that each adventure would translate into yet another book. Odd, that I, whose greatest ambition has always been the uninterrupted nap, should after all these years find himself the semi-famous author of several books!

And now we may have reached the final chapter. I must warn you that the story you are about to read is chilling, but it is one that nonetheless had to be told. I hope it will not disturb you or your readers too much, for it has never been my intention to disturb, merely to entertain. I trust you will find the entertainment value sufficiently present to warrant publication of this book as you have the others in the past.

I look forward to your response and, as always, I send you my good wishes.

Yours sincerely,
Harold X.

A curious letter, I thought. Then I began to read. And at once I understood why Harold had warned me the book would be disturbing. There on the very first page was another question. Would it remain unanswered? Read for yourself and ask as I did: Is this the end?

ONE

The End

HOW unexpectedly the end can come. Had I even thought such a thing was possible, I might have noticed the warning signs that Friday night one May when, ironically, I was feeling so at peace with the world. I remember the feeling well, for although a general sense of contentedness is part of a dog's nature, keen awareness of just how fortunate one is comes along less frequently than you might imagine. This was one of those rare moments.

I was stretched out on the bed next to my master, Toby. I call him my master because while there are four members of the Monroe family, it is the youngest who treats me with the greatest kindness and consideration. On Friday nights, for instance,

Toby, who is allowed to stay up late to read, shares his stash of treats with me. He knows how much I love chocolate, and so he's always sure to have at least one chocolaty delight ready and waiting for me. (Some of my readers have written expressing their concern about the potentially detrimental effects of chocolate on dogs, to which I can only say that while it is true some dogs have been known to become ill from eating chocolate, others have not. Luckily, I fall into the latter category. Also, I hasten to remind my readers that I, like the books I have written, am a work of fiction.)

Parenthetical digression aside, I return to that Friday evening in May when I lay happily snuggled up next to my favorite boy, my mouth blissfully tingling from the lingering taste of my favorite food—a chocolate cupcake with cream in the middle, yum. Toby's hand rested on my head, which in turn rested on his outstretched legs. The warm spring breeze wafted through the open window, gently carrying Toby's voice as he read to me. Toby is the kind of reader who devours books—and long books, at that—unlike his older brother, Pete, whose reading is limited to a series of truly gross horror novels called FleshCrawlers. (Believe me, I know they're gross; I chewed on one once and the cheap glue they use on the bindings made me sick as a—you should pardon the expression—dog. Give me Literature any day!)

Lulled by Toby's voice, I remember thinking how perfect my life seemed at that moment. My best friend, Chester, had undoubtedly settled himself in on the brown velvet armchair in the living room below and was now contentedly sleeping or shedding or reading. He, like Toby, is a voracious reader, which may surprise you, given that he's a cat; but, again, in the world of fiction, anything is possible. Consider the other two members of the Monroe menagerie: Howie, a wirehaired dachshund puppy who Chester maintains is part werewolf, and Bunnicula, a rabbit with fangs. While Chester doesn't concern himself much with Howie's howling, seeing it as irritating but harmless, he does work himself up into a fancy frenzy from time to time over the dangers he imagines Bunnicula poses to our vegetables, our family, the town in which we live, and, when he's really on a roll, Civilization as we know it.

Now all of this may seem very strange to you,

but to me it is just life. I couldn't picture it any other way. Over time, the eight of us in our family—four people, four pets—have settled into the comforting rhythms of a song without end. Or so I thought.

I had been only vaguely listening to the story Toby was reading. I knew that it was about the famous detective Sherlock Holmes and his friend Watson because those stories were all that Toby had been reading for weeks. I had grown fond of Holmes and had often thought that his friendship with Watson was something like mine with Chester. I was therefore unprepared for the terrible event that concluded this particular tale, in which Watson tells of the final confrontation between Holmes and his archenemy, the evil Professor Moriarty.

"'As I turned away I saw Holmes, with his back against a rock and his arms folded, gazing down at the rush of waters. It was the last that I was ever destined to see of him in this world,'" Toby read.

I lifted my head and woofed. Was it possible? Would Holmes perish? Could an author be so cruel as to kill off his most beloved character?

As if he could read my mind, Toby looked down at me with a forlorn expression on his face. "Are you worried about what's going to happen?" he asked. "I wish I could tell you the story has a happy ending, boy, but . . . Well, I guess I'd better just finish reading."

I listened attentively to every word. You may imagine my shock when it was revealed that Holmes and Moriarty, locked in a deadly embrace, tumbled from the precipice overlooking Reichenbach Falls into "that dreadful cauldron of swirling water and seething foam," where they were lost forever.

I couldn't believe it! The author had really done it! He had killed Sherlock Holmes! I would have written him an irate letter then and there if I'd known where the Monroes kept their stamps—and if it hadn't occurred to me that the author had been dead for three-quarters of a century.

I began to whimper and Toby, whose own eyes were glistening, bent over me and crooned, "There, there, boy. It's only a story." But Toby is a sensitive lad, and I knew that for him, as for me, there was something more here than a story. There was the painful recognition that all too quickly things can change. I didn't like it. I wanted my world to go on as it always had. I wanted to be sure that Friday nights would always mean treats with Toby, that Chester would always be my friend, that Bunnicula would always be in his cage by the living-room window, and that Howie would always, for reasons no one understands, call me Uncle Harold and Chester Pop.

I jumped down from Toby's bed with an urgent need to check downstairs and be sure that everything was in its proper place.

"Hey, where're you going, boy?" I heard Toby call. I turned back to give his hand a quick lick, then bounded from the room and down the stairs.

"Chester!" I cried out as I turned the corner from the hall into the living room. His chair was empty!

"Chester! Where are you?" I called into the darkened room.

As my eyes adjusted, I could see that Howie was not curled up under the coffee table where he should have been. Where was everybody? Thank goodness, Bunnicula at least was where he belonged, sitting in his cage, gazing out at the empty living room.

I trotted over to his cage and said hello. Slowly,

he turned his head in my direction, and had I known then what I would later learn, I would have seen the listlessness in the movement, might even have detected the lack of luster in his normally sparkly eyes. Do I only imagine it now, or was there something behind that glassy gaze that was saying, "Help me, Harold"? How easy it is to look back and see everything so differently.

At the time, I was just relieved he was there. I didn't pay him any more mind at that moment because the door to the kitchen creaked open just then and through it appeared Chester, licking his chops.

"Where *were* you?" I said, trying to sound less alarmed than I felt and failing miserably. "I called you and called you."

Chester parked himself next to me and nonchalantly turned his tongue's attention to the tip of his tail. "For heaven's sake, Harold, get a grip on yourself. I was in the kitchen having a little snack. Knowing your inability to go without food for less than five minutes at a stretch, I assumed you'd be joining me. Now what's all the excitement about?"

"Well, I, that is . . ." I let my sentence drop, feeling foolish all of a sudden to be so worked up over a mere story. I might have reminded myself of the many times Chester had not only worked himself up but practically turned the house upside down from his hysterical overreaction to something he'd read— but then Chester *is* a cat and prone to overreacting.

"It was just—just something I read," I told him.

He snickered. "I understand. The list of ingredients on candy wrappers can be alarming."

He chortled to himself as I tried to think of a speedy comeback. Unfortunately, I am notoriously slow at speedy comebacks, so I gave up the effort even as I silently rejoiced that this exchange was proof that life in the Monroe house was proceeding as usual.

If further proof was needed, Howie came skipping down the stairs, his toenails clicking wildly. He raced to our sides and skidded to a halt.

"Boy," he said breathlessly, "that was *so* scary!" The poor kid was quivering.

"What happened?" I asked.

I noticed that Chester had stopped bathing his tail and was staring intently at Howie. His eyes were sharp. His ears were perked. He was ready to make his move on whatever had so frightened the impressionable young puppy.

"W-well," Howie stammered, "there was this giant p-p-potato, see, and he ate up everything in the refrigerator and when seventh grader Billy-Bob Krenshaw went to get milk for his cereal—"

"Hold it right there!" Chester snapped. Howie, who always does what Chester tells him, froze, his jaw dropped open, and his tongue unfurled like a flag hanging off a porch on a windless Fourth of July.

"Are you talking about what I think you're talking about?" Chester went on.

We waited.

"You can move your mouth now," Chester said.

"Thanks," said Howie. "I was talking about FleshCrawlers number nineteen, *The Potato Has a Thousand Eyes*. I was reading it over Pete's shoulder. Until he told me I had to leave because I had breath like the bottom of a garbage pail, which I resent because I haven't been near the garbage for a whole week, not since that time the baby-sitter left the lid off, which reminds me—"

"Howie!"

"What, Pop?"

"Do you have a point to make here? Do you know what I mean by a point?"

"Yes, I have a point to make!" said Howie. "And what was your other question? Did I know what a point meant? Of course I do. I had an appointment just last week with the vet. Get it, Pop? Get it, Uncle Harold?"

Howie chuckled merrily while Chester began to fume. I could have cried at how normal everything was.

"My point," Howie said, "was that the story was really scary. Especially the part where Billy-Bob's pet is transformed into a french-fried poodle."

Chester shook his head in disgust. "Who writes this drivel?" he asked.

"Drivel?" said Howie. "I don't know what drivel is, but I can tell you one thing. M. T. Graves does not write drivel! Besides, it could really happen—you said so yourself, Pop."

"What could really happen?"

"Vegetables can be dangerous."

"I've always said that about spinach," I interjected.

"Don't you remember when you were worried that Bunnicula was attacking vegetables all over town, draining them of their juices, and you said the vegetables would turn into vampires, too? Remember, Pop? You had us going around staking them through their little veggie hearts with toothpicks!"

"Well . . ." said Chester. I couldn't tell if the memory was making him proud or embarrassed. He's often poised between the two. You know how cats are—you never know if they're going to make a cool move or a fool move, and most of the time neither do they.

Howie pressed on. "You *do* still think Bunnicula's a vampire, don't you?"

"Of course," Chester said.

"And you *do* think he's a danger to vegetables, right?"

Chester hesitated before speaking. "Let's just say, he used to be a danger. I don't think we have to worry about that any longer."

"What do you mean?" I asked. Then I remembered. "Oh, because the Monroes feed him a liquid diet, he no longer drains vegetables of their juices. Is that it?"

Chester's face took on an odd expression. "Let's just say the matter is under control, Harold. At last."

"But, Chester," I said, "Bunnicula hasn't attacked any vegetables since he escaped that time. Surely you're no longer worried about him."

"Oh, I'm no longer worried about him. No, I'm not worried at all."

And with that, he jumped up on the brown velvet armchair, bid us good night, and, after circling and pawing at the seat cushion for a good five minutes, proceeded to fall into a deep and seemingly untroubled sleep.

Howie and I meandered over to Bunnicula's cage.

"What do you think Pop meant about everything being under control?" Howie asked as we regarded our lethargic chum.

"Chester just likes to hear himself talk sometimes," I told Howie. "And he likes to believe that Bunnicula is a threat. But I don't think he'd do him any real harm. After all, he's one of the family."

Howie smiled. "My brother, the bunny," he said. "Hey, that reminds me, Uncle Harold. Did you read FleshCrawlers number thirty-three, *My Sister the Pickled Brain*? It is so cool. See, there's this girl named Laura-Lynn O'Flynn who has this twin sister, and one day she asks her to help her with this science experiment and something goes way wrong and the next thing you know . . ."

As Howie nattered on, I thought about what I'd said to him. Although I was pleased to find life carrying on as usual in the Monroe household, I was troubled that something might once again be fanning the spark of Chester's suspicions and animosity toward an innocent rabbit—one we called a friend. Did I really believe Chester would do Bunnicula no harm? After all, he *had* tried to destroy Bunnicula once. How far would he have gone? How far would he go now? I had no answers and I did not like where the questions were taking me.

It was only later that night when I was fast asleep that the pieces came together as they do in dreams—the lifeless look in Bunnicula's eyes, Chester's mysterious comments, and the disturbing scene from the story Toby had read to me earlier. Was it one thing in particular, or was it all of the pieces floating dreamlike through my slumber, that put the questions into my mind that would not go away: Might Chester and Bunnicula be headed for their own fateful plunge from the precipice? Could this be the end of Bunnicula?

TWO

The Terrible Truth About Chester

IF Saturdays at your house are anything like Saturdays at our house, let me offer you a little advice: Do not fall asleep at the bottom of the stairs. After all my Saturdays with the Monroes, you would think I would have known better. But now that I'm well into my middle years, I take the position that if you can't live recklessly on occasion, what's the point of it all? Unfortunately, sometimes the point of it all is that you get trampled.

As was the case on the Saturday morning in question. I had little time to think of the dreams that had disturbed my sleep the night before when I was startled awake by the sound of Pete and Toby yelling at each other. The accompanying rumble told me a stampede was in progress, and, sure enough, when I looked up and saw the Monroe brothers scrambling down the stairs, there were Pete's bare and dirty feet heading straight for me. As far as I could tell, this morning's altercation had something to do with a large piece of cardboard Pete was waving around over his head, which Toby was trying to get from him.

For the record, I do not move quickly in the morning.

For the record, Pete and Toby do.

It was no contest.

Oomph!

"Watch it, Harold!" Pete shouted as he landed on a part of me that was blessedly not fully awake yet.

"You could say you're sorry!" Toby yelled at his brother, stopping to pat me on the head.

"I just did!" Pete shot back. Apparently, Toby had forgotten that "Watch it!" is Pete's idea of an apology.

Chester wandered in as Pete and Toby continued their morning exercises.

"Give me that poster!" Toby shouted. "I made it!"

Pete waved the poster at Toby. Toby grabbed at it

and missed. Pete called his brother a word of one syllable. Toby volleyed with a compound noun. Pete retorted with a backhanded insult. Toby lobbed a high string of colorful adjectives capped by a perfectly executed oxymoron.

"Boys!" Mrs. Monroe shouted from the top of the stairs. "Enough!"

"Breakfast!" Mr. Monroe called cheerfully and obliviously from the kitchen.

"And the match goes to Toby," Chester commented as he licked a curled paw. "Nice wordplay."

"People are fascinating, aren't they, Chester?" I asked as we followed the boys and the enticing aroma of bacon into the kitchen. "All those words and they actually imagine they're communicating."

"I swear," said Chester, "if you waved a sign in their faces that said FEED ME BEFORE I FAINT, they'd ask if you needed to go outside. Speaking of signs, what did the poster say?"

"Speaking of feed-me-before-I-faint," I replied, "who cares what the poster said?"

In the kitchen, I joined Howie at Mr. Monroe's side to pant and whimper and look as pathetic as possible while Mr. Monroe forked bacon onto a plate.

"Subtlety, thy name is dog," Chester observed sarcastically.

I chose not to engage in what I knew would be yet another futile round in one of our oldest debates—Getting the Food from Their Hand to Your Mouth: Shameless Begging versus Haughty Disdain. Besides, now that I was feeling a little more awake (helped by the strip of bacon Mr. Monroe slipped me on the sly; one point for shameless begging), my dreams started coming back to me. Questions were forming themselves in my mind, questions I needed to ask Chester as soon as the opportunity presented itself.

"No more, Harold," I heard Mr. Monroe say. I was unaware that he had seated himself at the table, and I had moved from whimpering at his side to laying my head on his lap and looking up at him plaintively. It's amazing the things that happen on automatic.

"If you want more breakfast," he said, scratching the top of my head, "go look in your bowl. There's a surprise waiting for you."

Before you could say, "For me?" I was at my bowl, where I found freshly ground meat! One thing

I have to say about the Monroes, their lives may get busy, but they always think of their pets in special little ways. I've always said I have the best family anyone could have. Even if I do get stomped on by a certain person's dirty, smelly feet occasionally.

"We won't be home until late," I heard Mrs. Monroe saying. "Toby, will you be sure to leave Bunnicula's carrot juice for him so he'll have it when he wakes up?"

"Okay," said Toby, chewing. Then, "Bunnicula hasn't been looking so good, Mom. Do you think there's something wrong with him?"

"Now that you mention it," said Mrs. Monroe, "there has been a real change in his energy lately. Maybe we should take him to the vet."

"He's just fat and lazy," said Pete.

"Oh, that's nice," Toby said.

"Boys," Mr. Monroe murmured in that way he has of letting you know you're about to sail into treacherous waters and you'd better change course.

For a moment everyone fell silent. Then Mr. Monroe said, "He doesn't seem seriously ill. Maybe we'll take him to the vet on Monday. I don't see how we can fit it in today. We've got so much to do, what with the rally at the movie house and all."

"Like this dumb rally is going to make a difference," said Pete. "I don't see why we're wasting our time. They're going to tear the theater down on Tuesday whether we protest or not. It's a lost cause."

"Your mother and I have put months into fighting this demolition, Pete, you know that. That theater is not only very convenient, it's architecturally important and is a local landmark of sorts. We're not going to stop now. Decisions can still be overturned."

"Besides, if the theater *is* torn down," said Toby, "tonight's movie will be the last one shown there. Ever! We don't want to miss *that*, do we? It's so unfair. Now we're going to have to go all the way out to the mall to see movies."

"Big wazoo!" said Pete, rolling his eyes. If eyerolling were an Olympic event, Pete would be a gold medalist.

I didn't stick around to hear the rest of the conversation. Having thoroughly cleaned my dish, I retired to the living room to begin the important task of wondering where my next meal would come from. Howie and Chester joined me.

"Chester," I said.

"Are you going to tell me you're worried the Monroes will forget to put food in your dish before they leave?" he asked.

"I most certainly was not!" I replied indignantly. How did he always know?

There was something else I wanted to ask him, of course—something about what he'd said the night before—but I couldn't bring myself to ask it just then. I don't know why. Perhaps I didn't want to have to face the answer I suspected he would give me.

In any event, we weren't left in peace for long. Mr. and Mrs. Monroe began bustling about, which mostly meant piling things into their car, and it struck me that most Saturdays were composed of piling a lot things into the car in the morning and taking a lot of things out of the car in the after-noon. I never noticed if they were the same things or not, but I'd concluded long ago that it was just one of those bizarre human rituals destined not to make a great deal of sense. Meanwhile, Pete ap-plied himself seriously to the task of finding ever new and creative ways to be annoying, while Toby took Howie and me out for a morning romp. When we got back I went into immediate nap mode.

I was awakened some time later by the sound of Toby's voice, soft and close, and the feel of his arms around my neck.

"I'm worried about Bunnicula, boy," he whispered in my ear. "Keep an eye on him, will you? Gee, if anything ever happened to him . . ."

I whimpered sympathetically and Toby sighed.

"Good old Harold," he said. "At least I'd still have you."

A tennis ball bounced off the top of my head.

"Nice catch, Harold!" Pete shouted.

"Mom!" Toby bellowed.

Mrs. Monroe emerged from the kitchen, her arms full of posters similar to the one Pete had been carrying earlier. "Come on, you two," she said. "We're going to be late for the rally. And will you please stop fighting? What happened to that promise you made me on Mother's Day? It's not even two weeks and the two of you are going at each other like cats and dogs. What am I saying? Harold and Howie and Chester get along better than you do."

The car horn honked.

"Let's go," Mrs. Monroe said. "Your father is getting antsy."

Toby gave me another squeeze, and the family was gone.

Chester glared at me.

"What?" I said.

"Why did Toby say, 'At least I'd still have you,' Harold? Why didn't he say, 'At least I'd still have you *and Chester*'?"

"May I remind you that just yesterday you deposited a hairball in his sneaker?"

"That was hardly my fault! I thought it was Pete's sneaker."

"Good point," I said. "But still you can understand—"

"Yes, yes," said Chester, dropping to the floor and stretching out. Cats have more ways of changing the subject than kids have excuses for not doing their homework.

Seeing that the subject was changed, however, I decided this was the moment to find out the truth.

"Chester, you said something yesterday," I began.

"Yes, and I'm sorry, Harold. I never should have called you a mindless mutt."

"Oh, that," I said. "I wasn't talking about that."

"But it was unkind of me," Chester went on. "Not to mention redundant."

"It's all right, Chester. I don't even hear your insults anymore."

"You don't?"

Ignoring Chester's wounded look, I persevered. "You said that there was no need to worry about Bunnicula anymore, that the matter was under control. What did you mean by that?"

Chester smiled slyly. "I think you know what I mean. Sometimes it's best to leave certain things unsaid."

"But—"

Just then, Howie came bounding into the room. "Don't go in the yard!" he cried out, his voice full of alarm.

"What is it?" I woofed, racing to the window to see what was going on.

"I just finished reading FleshCrawlers number fifty-two, *Don't Go in the Yard*. It's about this boy named Skippy Sapworthy, who moves with his parents into this creepy old house and he's told never to go into the yard, but one night he—"

"Howie," Chester said.

"Yes, Pop?"

"The best way to overcome your fear is to face it. Why don't you and Harold run along and play outside for a while?"

"In the yard?"

"In the yard."

Howie looked at me. "Want to, Uncle Harold?" he asked.

"I wouldn't mind a little fresh air," I told him. "Coming, Chester?"

"Not just now," said Chester. "There's something I need to do. But don't let me stop you. Run along and play."

It was only moments later as Howie and I were tussling over an old rag in the backyard that Chester's words hit me.

"What fools!" I exclaimed. "Every day for the last few weeks, Chester has told us to run outside and play and, being the obedient dog-types we are, we do it! Howie, don't you see?"

Howie looked surprised by my question. "Of course I see, Uncle Harold," he said. "And I hear and I smell and I taste and I—"

"No, no. I mean, don't you see what Chester is up to? He's gotten us out of the house so he can, so he can . . ."

"So he can what?" Howie asked.

I looked at him blankly. "I don't know," I said, "but there's one way to find out."

As stealthily as we could, we made our way across the yard, through the pet door and into the kitchen, where we were stopped in our tracks by the strangest sound emanating from the living room.

Slurp, slurp, slurp.

Was it Bunnicula, sucking the juice out of vegetables? It couldn't be—he was never awake during daylight hours. Suddenly, the terrible truth hit me—it was Chester! Chester had become a vampire! He was sucking the lifeblood out of Bunnicula! That's why he said there was nothing to worry about anymore. That's why Bunnicula had become so listless! It was all too beastly to believe, too awful to face, yet I knew I must face it, must fling open the door that separated us, and put an end to Chester's hideous deeds!

"Be brave," I told young Howie, without explaining why he would need to be. How could I tell him what lay on the other side of that door, what violation of all that was good and decent accounted for those seemingly innocent slurping sounds?

"Now!" I said, and with Howie at my side, I butted the door open, charged into the living room, and cried out in wild desperation, "The game is up, Chester! I know you're a vampire! Let the bunny go!"

THREE

Do Not Litter!

"HAVE you completely lost your mind?" Chester asked.

Had I not worked myself up into such a state, I might have asked him the same thing. There he was inside Bunnicula's cage, all hunched up next to the sleeping rabbit, the hair and whiskers around his lips slick and matted with . . .

Carrot juice?

"Fine, so you're not a vampire," I said, trying to sound calm despite my heart's pounding reminder that I was anything but. "You *are* drinking Bunnicula's carrot juice, though, are you not?"

"Past tense, Harold. I just finished."

"Gee, Pop," said Howie, "there must be some

way to let the Monroes know you like carrot juice, too. You don't have to drink Bunnicula's."

"I don't like carrot juice, Howie," Chester said, gingerly stepping over the inert bunny and out of the cage. Carefully locking the door behind him, he jumped down and joined us. "I do not drink it for pleasure. I drink it because I must."

"Is that why you eat string?" I asked.

"I ate string once in my life, Harold. Leave it to you to remember."

"How could I forget? There you were with this little piece of string dangling from your lips and Mr. Monroe went to pull it out and he kept pulling and pulling, and the next thing you know he was clear across the other side of the room holding one end of a twenty-foot piece of string with your mouth still holding the other end. You looked like a tape dispenser."

Howie cracked up. Chester did not.

"But that's beside the point," I said. "The point is, why are you doing this?"

Chester sighed heavily. "Harold," he said, "you have a touching belief in the goodness of all creatures great and small. But how many times do I have to tell you? Bunnicula is not like other rabbits. He is evil."

"Now, Chester," I said.

"Tut, Harold, don't interrupt. You asked me for the truth, and now you will hear the truth."

Howie lowered his rear end to the floor, an indication that he was settling in for a good story. I wondered if he understood the distinction between fiction and reality. Then again, I suspected that for Chester there was no distinction at all.

"It began about a month ago," Chester said. "It was a Saturday. I remember it particularly because Mr. and Mrs. Monroe had received phone calls that morning from both their mothers that they would be coming to visit on Mother's Day. And although Mother's Day was still two weeks away, the family spent the rest of the day in a frenzy of cleaning and fixing up and telling us we were underfoot and—"

"Piling things in the car and taking things out. Yes, I remember," I said.

"And we ended up getting kicked out of the house," Howie put in, "and they forgot about us and it started to rain and—"

"Yes, it was a memorable day," said Chester. "Well,

Bunnicula slept through the day, of course, as he always does, but in the middle of the following night I was awakened by a clicking sound in the kitchen, followed by a light appearing under the door."

"Refrigerator," I surmised.

"Precisely. I might have made nothing of it had I not happened to glance in the direction of Bunnicula's cage and seen that it was empty. Well, what was I to think, Harold? He was at it again! He was in there, I had no doubt of it, attacking artichokes, sucking squash, biting broccoli, sinking his fangs into fennel—"

"Stop!" Howie cried. "It's too horrible!"

Chester pressed on relentlessly. "I tried to catch him in the act, but, oh, he's a tricky devil, that one, and he outmaneuvered me. By the time I entered the kitchen, he was gone. He had left his victims behind, though, carelessly scattered about the floor like so much litter on a public beach."

"Uncle Harold," Howie said, "when you write a book about this, will you find a way to remind your readers that they should never litter?"

"I definitely will," I promised. "Now go on, Chester."

"What was I to do? Should I leave those poor victimized victuals on the floor for the Monroes to discover in the morning? Remembering how dense they had been the first time this happened and, seeing no reason to think they'd grown any additional brain cells since then, I decided on a different course of action. I buried the pallid produce under some other garbage in the pail and made a vow to myself once and for all to take matters into my own hands."

"Paws," Howie said.

"Why?" asked Chester. "Do you need to go get a drink of water?"

"Take matters into your own paws. You don't have hands."

Chester pulled his lips back into a strained smile. "Has anyone ever told you you're a bright little whippersnapper?" he asked.

"Gee, no," Howie said, beaming.

"Well, there's a reason for that," Chester said, and then he went on. "Every night for the next two weeks it was the same thing. Out of his cage, into the kitchen, drain the veggies, and back before dawn. But I detected a puzzling difference from times past when Bunnicula had sucked the juice out of vegetables. This time he didn't always finish the job. It must be, I thought, that he isn't all that hungry. After all, he was still drinking the juice the Monroes gave him every day. What then was his motive? It almost appeared that he was playing a game, that attacking vegetables was a form of sport for him. I thought about it, and it occurred to me that Bunnicula was unusually frisky and playful at that time."

Although I wondered why neither Howie nor I had come upon any evidence of these nighttime escapades, I knew the last part of what Chester had said was true. I remembered how on several occasions when Toby and Pete had taken Bunnicula out of his cage, he'd frolicked about with enormous energy and had appeared especially contented when he'd cuddled into the crook of Toby's neck. As best one can judge the emotional state of a rabbit, I would have said he was the happiest I'd ever known him.

"But he's not like that anymore," I pointed out. "When did it change? And why?"

"This is where the story becomes truly curious," Chester replied. "A couple of weeks ago, I was all set to prevent his midnight runs on the refrigerator when—"

Howie interrupted. "How were you going to do that, Pop?"

"Garlic," Chester said matter-of-factly. "It immobilizes vampires and, as Harold can tell you, it's worked on Bunnicula in the past. In any event, I never got to use it because all of a sudden he stopped."

"No more sinking his fangs into fennel?" Howie asked.

"No more attacking artichokes," said Chester.

"So why didn't you just leave him alone?" I inquired.

"At first, I thought I might. Then it occurred to me that he was probably well aware of my watching him. What if he was trying to lull me into a false sense of security? Perhaps he had something really *big* planned. Ha! I thought. I'll show him a thing or two! And with that, I began sneaking into his cage every day and drinking that disgusting potion the Monroes concoct for him. And as you can see, he's gotten weaker and weaker."

And you, Chester, I thought, have gotten weirder and weirder.

"Do you intend to continue to deprive him of his food until he starves?" I asked.

Chester just gazed at me slyly.

"Let me just repeat: The matter is now under control," he said.

So at the very least Chester planned to keep Bunnicula at bay by weakening him. Yet I couldn't help thinking that there was another reason Bunnicula had stopped his attacks, a reason beyond lack of food, that he had suddenly become less frisky, a reason that had nothing to do with Chester. However, my dog's brain, which is to a cat's brain what a corridor is to a labyrinth, could not begin to sort it all out. No, it would take Chester to do that—and although the conclusion he would draw would be based more on a hunch than hard, cold fact, it would prove to be correct. Just as the consequences would prove to be nearly catastrophic.

FOUR

A Rabbit's Tears

I DID not sleep well that night. Toby tossed and turned, and I, tethered to the end of his bed by inertia, allowed myself to be rolled this way and that until shortly before dawn when he sat up and whispered in the dark, "Harold, are you awake?" Not waiting for an answer, he climbed out from under his covers and wrapped himself around me in a full body hug.

"I had bad dreams, boy," he said in a hushed tone. "Did I tell you what movie we saw last night when we went to the last show at the theater? *Dracula.* Not the new one we saw the time we found Bunnicula, but the old one with Bela Lugosi. It wasn't even in color and the special effects were totally lame. I didn't think it was scary at all when I was watching it, but, boy,

Harold, it sure was scary in my dreams."

I looked him in the eye and panted to let him know I understood.

"Aw, you understand, don't you, boy?" he said.

Works every time.

"I'll tell you one thing, Harold," he said, yawning. "You'd better stay out of Mom and Dad's way today. They're pretty bummed out about this theater thing, losing the battle and all. You know what's going to happen on Tuesday? Boom! They're coming in with a wrecking ball and down it goes!"

He yawned again. "Well, I'm going to try to get some more sleep. What are you going to do?"

He ruffled the hair on the top of my head, then crawled back under the covers, and before I'd had time to find out if his question was multiple choice or essay, he was sound asleep.

Looking out the window, I could see that the sky was beginning to grow light. Bunnicula, whose sleeping and waking hours were at odds with everyone else's in the house, would be going to sleep soon for the day, and that meant it was time for his old buddy Harold to sing him a lullaby.

As quietly as I could, I removed myself from

Toby's bed, stretched out my aching muscles, and lumbered down the stairs.

On first encountering the familiar scene in the living room, I felt immensely reassured. Bunnicula was in his cage, Chester was curled up in his armchair, Howie lay sprawled under the coffee table. Each was in his proper place. Serenity was spread over the room like cream cheese on a bagel.

Now for those of you who haven't read my first book, *Bunnicula*, the idea of my singing a lullaby to my little furry friend in the language of his native land (a remote area of the Carpathian Mountains region) may strike you as peculiar. For those of you who have read the book, the idea probably strikes you as just as peculiar, but at least you've been warned. You see, soon after Bunnicula's arrival in our home, I discovered that this particular lullaby soothes him, and so I have sung it to him regularly ever since. Roughly translated, it goes something like this:

> *The sheep are in the meadow,*
> *The goats are on the roof,*
> *In the parlor are the peasants,*
> *In the pudding is the proof.*

Dance on the straw
And laugh at the moon
Night is heavy on your eyes
And morning will come soon.

So sleep, little baby,
There's nothing you should fear,
With garlic at the window
And your mama always near.

Admittedly, it sounds better in the original. I only regret that I cannot record the melody here, for there is a wistful melancholia about it that would touch you, I'm certain, as it touches me when I croon it in my throaty baritone. And I know it touches Bunnicula as it carries him off to dreamland. On this occasion, however, I noted a new response on Bunnicula's part—one that struck me as curious and, under the circumstances, somewhat alarming.

"Do rabbits cry?" I asked Chester after Bunnicula had fallen asleep.

Chester had roused himself from his night's slumber and was in the middle of doing that stretch cats do where they extend their front paws out on the floor in front of them as if they're praying and

raise their rear ends up high like they're waiting for the whole world to notice and say, "Hey, that's some nice tush you got there."

I explained that as I was singing the lullaby to Bunnicula—the same one, I pointed out, that I'd sung him many times before—tears were rolling down his fuzzy little cheeks.

"Rabbits don't have a sentimental bone in their bodies," Chester said, dismissing the whole thing categorically. "Especially vampire rabbits."

And with that he marched into the kitchen for breakfast. End of discussion.

I glanced out the window. The sky was gray, and a misty rain was beginning to fall. The perfect sort of day for serious napping, I thought, and that was exactly how I intended to spend it.

And that was exactly how I *was* spending it until some time later when I heard Chester's voice buzzing in my ear like a gnat.

"Harold, Harold," he buzzed. "I know you're in there, Harold!"

What next? I thought. We've got you surrounded?

"Okay, fine," he went on, "it takes you time to open your eyes, I know that. I wouldn't want you to strain yourself, have a heart attack or something, from the effort of pushing up your eyelids too quickly, so just listen."

Do I bite him now or later?

"I've got it all figured out, Harold."

"He does, Uncle Harold, he really does."

Oh, joy. The junior detective is also on the scene.

"Howie, let me handle this, will you?" Chester said.

"Sure, Pop."

I began to snore.

"Stop trying to pretend you're asleep, Harold," Chester pressed on relentlessly. "Okay, here's my theory. First, when was it that Bunnicula started acting frisky and playful and when, not so coincidentally, did he start his most recent assault on vegetables? Right after Mr. and Mrs. Monroe received calls from their mothers, that's when. Now, when did everything change? Two weeks later, on Mother's Day, Harold! When he heard the other mothers were coming, he must have gotten it into his little hare brain that *his* long-lost mother might be coming on Mother's Day, too, and when she didn't . . . it was down-in-the-dumps for our little furry friend."

"I'll bet he thinks she doesn't love him anymore," Howie chimed in. "And you know what they say—you're no bunny till some bunny loves you."

Fascinating. I could actually *hear* Chester gritting his teeth. "What more evidence do you need, Harold? Think about it. He *cried* when you sang him that silly lullaby. He cried, Harold. He misses his mother! But that's not the half of it. He has plans, Harold, I'm sure of it. Some of those tears were because his plans were not fulfilled. Come on, let's go. I know that you know that I know what must be done!"

Slowly, I raised my eyelids. "Do you talk that

way just to drive me crazy?" I asked. "Or do you actually *think* in sentences like that?"

"If there's any chance Bunnicula's mother has returned, we've got to find her before he does," Chester said.

"Before he does," Howie echoed.

"It can't all be coincidence, Harold. Just think about it. Mother's Day . . . and what movie was playing at the theater? *Dracula,* Harold, *Dracula!*"

I looked at the two of them. I looked out the window. I thought back to Chester's description of Bunnicula's half-finished attacks on the vegetables, as if it were a sport. Maybe he was celebrating in his own way the possibility of being reunited with his mother. There was some logic to that.

"But it's raining," I pointed out.

"So?" said Chester. "You're waterproof. If Bunnicula's mother is out there, who knows how many more vampire rabbits are on the loose?"

"Okay, okay, I'll go with you," I said. "Just give me a minute to look for my mind, will you? I seem to have lost it."

Luckily—at least, luckily for Chester and

Howie—the Monroes were all in other parts of the house, so they didn't see us sneaking out the pet door into the rain.

"This is so cool," Howie yipped excitedly as we rounded the corner at the end of the block. "It's just like FleshCrawlers number twenty-four, *My Parents Are Aliens from the Planet Zorg*. See, there's this girl named Tiffani-Sue Tribellini, and she's trying to find her mother because the person she thinks is her mother is really an alien. How the girl knows is that every time her mother goes near the microwave she glows. Which is not your normal mother thing to do. So one day—"

"Will you two get a move on?" Chester scolded.

"Chester!" I shouted back. "Do you have a clue where you're leading us?"

"More than a clue! We're going to the last place Bunnicula saw his mother and where I believe we will now find her, waiting for her sonny boy! The movie theater!"

"Oh, goody!" Howie cried out. "Can we get popcorn? Can I sit on the aisle? Will there be coming attractions?"

I didn't have the heart to tell Howie we weren't actually going to see a movie. As it turned out, we never even got to the theater. With the disaster that would soon befall us, I couldn't help thinking I'd been right in the first place. It was a perfect day for napping.

FIVE

Surprise Encounters

A BIT of an explanation may be useful here. Those of you whose memory, like mine, is as full of holes as a garden hose after Howie's played Let's-Pretend-This-Long-Green-Thing's-a-Snake with it may not recall the exact circumstances of Bunnicula's coming to live with us. One night a couple of years ago, the Monroes went to the movies and on one of the seats discovered a dirt-filled shoebox holding a tiny white-and-black bunny. A note in a foreign language read TAKE GOOD CARE OF MY BABY. Because the movie *Dracula* was playing there that night, Mrs. Monroe had the bright idea of combining "bunny" and "Dracula" to come up with the rabbit's name: Bunnicula. This was after she'd had the anything-but-bright ideas of naming him Fluffy or Bun-Bun. She means well, Mrs. Monroe, but sometimes her taste is decidedly *Brady Bunch*.

Now I was not convinced, as Chester clearly was, that Bunnicula's mother—if she in fact had been the one to leave him at the movie theater in the first place—would still be hanging around there. After all, how long could anybody take a diet of stale popcorn and gummy bears? And if she had not stayed there, what would make her want to return? Remorse? But I did find his argument compelling that Bunnicula, for whatever reason, seemed to miss his mother and had gone on his recent rampage out of excitement over Mother's Day. So perhaps it was worth trying to find her. I didn't let on that my motives were different from his. He may have been out to undo some vague grand plan he imagined was under way. He may have been determined to destroy vampire rabbits. *I* was intent on reuniting them.

Luckily, the rain stopped, the sun came out, and soon the sweet smell of spring blossoms and fresh earth permeated the air. Not to mention certain other aromas of infinitely greater interest to dogs.

"Do you two have to stop at *every* hydrant?" Chester snapped at one point.

"We're investigating," I explained.

"Yeah," said Howie, "maybe we'll pick up Bunnicula's mother's scent."

"Unless she's a volunteer firerabbit, I don't think that's too likely," Chester retorted. "Now, come on!"

"How do you know where the movie theater is?" I called out.

"I don't!" Chester shot back.

I would have protested, but what difference would it have made? Chester never allows a minor detail like not knowing where he's going to get in his way. Besides, it really was shaping up to be a beautiful day and, to my surprise, I was glad to be out in it. I didn't even mind that the streets we were trotting along no longer seemed familiar.

After some time, we came to a street that was lined with stores. A new scent caught the attention of my nostrils. I lifted them to the air and sniffed.

"Pizza!" I cried. "Lunchtime!"

"No anchovies on mine," said Howie. I doubted he knew what anchovies were. He just said it, I think, because Pete always says it when the Monroes order pizza.

"Will you two get your minds off your stomachs for once?" Chester said impatiently. "Look at those two dogs over there. They seem perfectly content just to be lying in the sun. Why can't the two of you—"

Chester was cut off by Howie's yipping, "It's Bob and Linda!"

I looked closely. A caramel-colored cocker spaniel in a Mets cap. A West Highland white terrier with a lavender bandanna knotted jauntily around her neck. The bandanna may have been different, but otherwise the two looked exactly the same as when we'd last seen them.

"It *is* them!" I exclaimed. "Chester, it's Bob and Linda from Chateau Bow-Wow."

I don't know whether it was Bob and Linda in particular or the memory of the boarding kennel where we'd met them, but Chester muttered, "Oh, no," and rolled his eyes. If Pete was an Olympic eye-roller, Chester could have been his coach.

Howie ran on ahead of us.

"Well, look who it is," I heard Bob saying. "Linda, it's little Howie from that dreadful place the kids left us last summer." "The kids" was what Bob and Linda called their owners.

Linda raised herself to her haunches. "Well, so it is!" she remarked. Looking in my direction, she called out, "Yoo-hoo, Harold, is that you?"

"And Chester," I called back. Chester was muttering under his breath as we approached.

"Well, for heaven's sake," Linda went on, "whatever brings you to Upper Centerville? This is just too quaint."

I noticed that the two dogs were tied to a parking meter in front of a coffee place called ESPRESSO YOURSELF. Bob's leash was bright green with the word POLO printed repeatedly in purple letters along its length. Linda's was lavender (perfectly matching her bandanna) with HALSTON repeated on it in black. Next to them was a ceramic trough with *Pour les chiens* written on its side. It was filled with water with slices of lemon floating in it. I later learned that *pour les chiens* means "for the dogs."

So this was Upper Centerville.

"Well," I said, trying to come up with an answer to Linda's question that would not immediately

qualify us for the loony bin, "we're out for a stroll, actually. We, we . . ."

"We're looking for the movie theater," Chester said.

What a relief! He wasn't going to say . . .

"Because . . ."

Oh, no.

". . . we're looking for a vampire rabbit. Have you seen one?"

"Uh, not lately," said Bob. He looked over his shoulder as if to say, "I wonder what's keeping the kids."

"We don't get many vampire rabbits in Upper Centerville," Linda said, regarding Chester with a mixture of sympathy and distaste. "What exactly would we be looking for?"

"Black and white," said Chester. "Red eyes. Fangs. Strange eating habits."

They thought for a moment. "We *do* know a dalmatian who's awfully fond of Tofutti," Linda offered.

"But then who isn't?" said Bob.

Linda nodded her head as Chester began muttering to himself again.

"I wish the kids would get out here with our cappuccino," Bob said. Then, "Say, here's a coincidence. We ran into two other inmates—I mean, guests—from Chateau Bow-Wow just the other day."

Linda wrinkled her nose. "Those two *cats*," she said. "No offense to you, Chester."

"None taken," said Chester. "I assume you're referring to Felony and Miss Demeanor."

"Indeed," said Bob. "Seems they were up to their old tricks. The kids were walking us in downtown Centerville. They hadn't taken us there in years, but now it's so 'out' it's 'in' again, if you know what I mean."

I didn't have a clue.

Linda picked up the story. "We had just passed the movie theater when we spotted these two cats scurrying out from behind a garbage pail in the next alley. I referred to them as riffraff—a little loudly, I'm afraid—and one of them said, 'Hey, you remember us!' and that's when I knew it had to be—"

"Felony and Miss Demeanor," said Bob. "They seemed genuinely pleased to see us. They asked where we lived."

"We told them we'd just moved and couldn't remember the address," Linda said. "After all, they *are* cat burglars. They were on their way to a so-called caper even as we spoke. Shameful."

Bob shook his head sadly. "They have too much time on their hands, that's their problem. They need a hobby. Anyway, they told us they lived down there."

"In the alley?" Chester asked.

"No," said Linda, "somewhere nearby. They just use the alley as their office."

"Wow," said Howie, "do they have a fax machine?"

Bob smiled indulgently at Howie. "I don't think so," he said. "Maybe you'll see them when you go to the movie theater."

"There's something to live for," said Chester.

As he was getting directions to downtown Centerville, Linda suddenly remembered something.

"Last night," she said, "we saw a black-and-white animal rummaging about in the garbage behind that new vegetarian restaurant. Just caught a glimpse of it really. Maybe it was the rabbit you're looking for."

Chester's ears perked up. "Vegetarian, did you say?"

"Yes, it's right down the street here between

Maison de Wallpaper and Amour de Hair; you can't miss it."

"In the French Quarter, eh?" said Chester. "Well, thanks for the tip. We'll check it out before we head downtown to the theater."

Bidding Bob and Linda goodbye, we headed off down the street.

"If it *was* Bunnicula's mother," said Howie as Maison de Wallpaper came into view, "wouldn't she be asleep now?"

"Making it all the easier for us to find her," said Chester, a satisfied smile creeping across his face. "Who knows? Maybe we'll get lucky and find more than one sleeping vampire rabbit! There, that must be it!"

VICIOUSLY VEGGIE, the sign on the restaurant read. POWER FOOD FOR THE POWER HUNGRY. I was learning a lot about the people who lived in Upper Centerville.

A narrow passageway ran between the two buildings. We could make out a glimpse of garbage cans and what looked like a Dumpster at the far end.

Chester went into his skulking position.

"Oh, do we *have* to?" I whined. "You know I hate to skulk."

"You're a hunter!" Chester snapped. "Now let's go!"

Chester began to slink along the building's edge, his body tight and as focused as a missile homing in on its target. I would have taken him a little more seriously had I not seen him assume this same position stalking a butterfly the week before.

Howie was directly behind Chester, imitating his every move. For sheer entertainment value, there's nothing quite like watching a dachshund try to slink like a cat.

But who am I to judge? After all, was I not soon third in line? If I wasn't exactly skulking, I was doing some sort of vague interpretation of your basic hunting stance. Not that I've ever *been* a hunting dog, mind you, regardless of what Chester may think about my canine instincts. The Monroes don't believe in hunting, for one thing, and as for me, just the thought of carrying something dead and uncooked between my teeth . . . *brrr.*

As we got closer to the back of the buildings, Chester slowed to a near halt.

"I see something," he hissed. "Look there, between those two garbage cans."

I didn't see a thing until the sun bounced off something shiny. Was it metal? No, it glistened and moved as if it was alive.

"I'm going to go in for a closer look," said Chester. "Cover me."

"Okay," Howie said. "Do we have a blanket, Uncle Harold?"

"I don't think that's what Chester has in mind."

"Oh."

Chester was moving as cats do when they're closing in on their prey, which is to say I could have napped between steps. When he got close, however, his demeanor—and his tempo—did an abrupt change.

"Run!" he shouted as he turned and sped past us back up the alleyway.

"What is it?" I cried out.

Well may you ask why I cried out instead of following Chester's (for once) wise advice. Suffice it to say that those three little words kept me in the wrong place for three little seconds too long.

And then it was all over. All over Howie. And all over me.

We hightailed it out of there as fast as we could, but the damage was done. My eyes were stinging. My throat was burning. My nostrils were begging for mercy.

"Chester!" I shouted. "I'm going to get you for this!"

But Chester couldn't hear me. He was far off in the distance, heading for home. So was Howie. And so was I.

And so was the stench of a *skunk*.

SIX

Tomato Juice, Togas, and Trouble

IF Pete said "Gross!" once, he said it a hundred times.

I tried not taking it personally. After all, it *was* pretty gross. Not to mention humiliating. Especially when Mr. Monroe bathed Howie and me in tomato juice. Chester had managed to escape the skunk's assault, but Mr. Monroe considered giving him a regular bath just to be on the safe side. Knowing how much Chester hates baths, he spelled it out.

"I think I should give Chester a b-a-t-h, too," he told Mrs. Monroe.

To which Chester's response was, "I'm out of h-e-r-e," and he was gone.

The Monroes haven't figured out that Chester can spell.

Cats, in case you don't know it, do not care to be bathed by anything other than their own tongues. Dogs, on the other hand, have an entirely different philosophy of life. Simply stated, it's this: Never do for yourself what you can get others to do for you. I call this "conservation of energy." Chester has a less exalted name for it. "Laziness," I believe it is.

In any event, after our tomato juice baths, Howie and I were plunked in the tub for a nice long soak. Howie got to practice his backstroke and I got to practice my lifesaving skills each time he sank to the bottom.

It was after Mr. Monroe had left us swathed in towels to dry off that Chester poked his head around the bathroom door, looked to the left and right, sniffed the air to be sure we no longer stank, and cautiously entered the room.

"Chester," I said, "I'd like a few words with you."

"All right, all right," he said, "so Plan A didn't exactly work out."

"It didn't exactly work out?" I repeated. "Is that all you have to say for yourself?"

"No," said Chester. "I also want to tell you about Plan B."

I am not normally prone to violence, but at that moment I might have been tempted to tie Chester's whiskers in a bountiful array of knots had I not been so tightly wrapped in my towel. At the very least I would have pressed for an apology, but I was beginning to see that there were more similarities between Chester and Pete than I'd ever noticed before. Being a cat or an eleven-year-old boy, I surmised, must mean never having to say you're sorry.

"Okay, lads, here's what I'm thinking," Chester said as he began to pace in front of us. Howie loves it when Chester gets going like this and he panted appreciatively. I, on the other hand, tried rolling my eyes but only succeeded in noticing that my bangs needed trimming.

"Let's say I'm right about Bunnicula's mother," Chester said, "which of course I am. My guess is that Bunnicula hasn't figured out where she is. Maybe he hasn't even made the connection between his mother and the movie theater. Otherwise, he would have broken out of this joint a long time ago.

So he's still waiting for her to come to him. Fine. Here's what we've got to do."

He paused to look at us.

"Why do I feel like I'm addressing the Roman Senate?" he asked.

Howie and I looked blankly at each other.

"Is that a trick question?" Howie said.

Chester shook his head wearily. "Togas," he said. "You look like you're wearing togas. The way they did in ancient Rome. Don't you two ever read?"

He should have known better than to ask.

"I read a book about ancient Rome!" Howie piped up enthusiastically. "*Screaming Mummies of the Pharaoh's Tomb.* FleshCrawlers, number twenty-eight. There were these twins, see, Harry and Carrie Fishbein, and they found this time-travel machine in their grandfather's attic. They were just fooling around with it, but before you knew it—*poof!*—they were in ancient—"

"Egypt!" Chester snapped, cutting Howie off. "They were in ancient Egypt, Howie, and the two of you look like ancient Romans, and there is an actual difference between ancient Egypt and ancient Rome, and why I even bother to bring up historical or literary references with you two dolts is beyond me!"

Chester kept on ranting, but I'm not sure what else he had to say. Drowsy from my bath and the room's warmth, I nodded off somewhere around "historical or literary references." When I regained consciousness, he was carrying on about Plan B.

"So we've got to keep our eye on him at all times," he was saying, "because if he does start making connections, there's no stopping him. Either we have to prevent their reuniting entirely or, better yet, use Bunnicula to lead us to his mother. He may still be weak, but even so I'm going to need your help. Maybe we should work in shifts."

"We have to put on *dresses?*" Howie whined.

Chester grimaced. "We'll *take turns,* okay?"

"Oh."

Just then, Mr. Monroe came into the room to give us a final rubdown. He looked at us and smiled.

"Chester, you look like you're addressing the Roman Senate," he said.

"Uncanny," Chester commented after Mr. Monroe had left.

"Yes," I said, thinking of yesterday's breakfast, "it was nice having fresh meat for a change, wasn't it?"

"Hey, Uncle Harold," Howie said. "I get it. Fresh meat. Uncanny. That was pretty good."

"Thanks, Howie," I said, leaving it at that. It's embarrassing when you make a joke and don't even realize it.

The night watch began. Why I was supporting Chester's harebrained scheme I don't know. Sometimes you just find yourself doing things Chester expects you to do. So I volunteered to take the first shift, figuring that it would be better to get it over with and have the rest of the night for uninter-rupted sleep. What I hadn't counted on was the dis-covery I would make while I was on duty, one that would keep me awake—and alert—the whole night.

Bunnicula was sick. Really sick. Far weaker than he would be from Chester's depriving him of his carrot juice. He wasn't moving at all. When I talked to him, his ears didn't twitch or stir as they normally did. At times, it seemed he wasn't even breathing.

Not wanting to alarm Howie, I let him sleep through his shift. As for Chester, well, I tried to con-vince him that Bunnicula was in trouble, but he wasn't having any of it.

"Either he misses his mother or he's faking" was his unscientifically arrived at diagnosis. "Neither one is fatal, Harold. And if it is—"

"Chester! What are you saying?"

"I think you know what I'm saying, Harold."

Desperately seeking some way of comprehend-ing Chester's devious mind, I asked, "Chester, are you still drinking Bunnicula's juice?"

"Not all the time," he answered, "although I have developed a taste for the stuff. No, I have other ways of foiling his plans now."

"But, Chester, he may be really sick," I said.

"Harold, once and for all, you've got to understand. Bunnicula is *not* the Easter bunny. He's a spinach sucker! The bane of broccoli! A bad rabbit with bad habits! If he can lead us to his mother, we may be able to put an end to this race of terrorizing hares once and for all!"

"But, Chester, you said yourself, he probably hasn't made any connections yet, and he certainly isn't going anywhere. He can barely move. How is he going to lead us to his mother when he can't lift his head?"

Chester narrowed his eyes to slits. "Don't underestimate his vampirical powers. Believe me, Harold, if he can't lead us to his mother, he will somehow manage to bring his mother here to him. You can lead a horse of a different color to water but it's still a horse."

Don't ask.

As it turned out, Bunnicula did go somewhere, but it was not under his own powers—vampirical or otherwise.

Unable to stand it any longer, I woke Toby just

before dawn and dragged him by the sleeve of his pajamas downstairs to Bunnicula's cage. It didn't take him long to get the picture.

"Mom! Dad! Come quick!" he shouted. "Bunnicula's really sick! I think he's going to die!"

Mr. and Mrs. Monroe raced down the stairs. Mr. Monroe, still half asleep, tumbled over the armchair, which sent Chester flying. Chester's indignant screech in turn woke Howie, who bolted from under the coffee table just in time to get tangled in Mr. Monroe's legs. Nobody, other than Chester, seemed to notice or care, though. All eyes were on Bunnicula.

"Oh, Robert," said Mrs. Monroe, touching her husband's arm as he opened the cage and lifted the limp, languid rabbit from it. "I *knew* we should have taken him to the vet on Saturday. We've waited too long."

Mr. Monroe held Bunnicula close to his chest. "His breathing seems normal, if a bit slow," he said, stroking the bunny lovingly. "But there's definitely something wrong with him. I'll call Dr. Greenbriar right away and leave a message that I'm bringing

Bunnicula in on my way to work this morning. I'm pretty sure his downtown office is open early on Mondays."

"Can I go with you, Dad?" Toby asked.

Mr. Monroe shook his head. "You have school today, young man."

"But I could miss it, couldn't I? What's one day of school?"

"You have tomorrow off because of teacher conferences. That's enough days off for this week. Besides, it's Bunnicula who's sick, not you."

"But what if Bunnicula d—" Toby stopped himself from completing his sentence. I bumped up against his leg to remind him that his pal Harold was there for him. I felt his hand come to rest lightly on the top of my head.

"Now, son," Mr. Monroe said in a soft, soothing voice, "I'm sure Bunnicula will be fine. Maybe there's a problem with the food we've been giving him. Or maybe it's some kind of virus. Whatever it is, Dr. Greenbriar will figure it out and have him all fixed up in no time flat."

"Promise?" Toby said.

I looked up at Mr. Monroe's face. There was

something in it that told me he wasn't entirely comfortable with his answer.

"Promise," he told Toby.

Later that morning, after Mr. and Mrs. Monroe had gone to work and Toby and Pete to school, the phone rang.

Howie jumped up from where he was napping and began running in circles. "I'll get it! I'll get it!" he yipped.

The answering machine picked up.

"Boys," Mr. Monroe's voice said. Howie stopped yipping at once. "I just wanted to leave you this message since you'll get home before I do today. Dr. Greenbriar is keeping Bunnicula overnight. He needs to run some tests. The important thing is not to worry. Bunnicula will be fine, guys. Okay? Bunnicula will be . . . fine."

The machine clicked off.

"Mr. Monroe didn't sound like Bunnicula would be fine," Howie said.

"No, he didn't," I agreed.

Chester said nothing, and the three of us fell into an uneasy silence. The only sound was the ticking of the grandfather clock in the hall. The space by the window where Bunnicula's cage had been sitting only that morning was empty, save for the fine layer of dust that held a few white and black hairs. I sniffed at them, sneezed from the dust, then felt my eyes grow wet with the thought that these few hairs were all that remained of Bunnicula. I'd never even said good-bye.

I turned. Chester was staring intently at the empty space.

"Plan C," he said, and then fell silent again.

SEVEN

Plant, See?

I DIDN'T see Chester for most of the rest of the day. I assumed he was keeping himself busy with Plan C, whatever that was, but since Bunnicula was now safely out of the house, I didn't worry about it much. Surely Dr. Greenbriar would find out what was wrong with him. And there would be no crazed cat around to suck down his vegetable juices while he slept, so at the very least Bunnicula would be able to eat properly again.

By the time the boys came home, I had begun to wonder where Chester was, however. On Mondays, Toby and Pete get home about a half hour before their father arrives from the university where he teaches. Howie and I always rush to the door to greet them and Toby always says, "Hi, guys, I'll bet you're hungry!"

Does he know dogs or what?

Now Chester may harp at me and Howie about our thinking with our stomachs, but it's a known fact that cats are every bit as meal-minded as dogs. It's just that dogs are more obvious about it. You take one look in our eyes and you know what we're thinking.

Feed me.

Pet me.

Love me.

Even if I did turn your new catcher's mitt into an unrecognizable glob of leather and dog slobber, I'm still your best buddy, right?

Cats, on the other hand, like to keep you guessing. They'll rub back and forth against your legs (I've observed that Chester likes to do this most when the Monroes are wearing black pants), meowing like crazy until you finally get the message, and then they start doing this little dance that you *think* is saying, "Yes, yes, that's it! Food! That's what I want! Give me food!" You bend down to put the bowl on the floor, and they practically knock you over trying to get at it. And then what happens? One sniff and they walk out of the kitchen with their tails in the air, as if to say, "Is *that* what you thought I wanted? You *must* be joking!"

I'm sure you have observed, however, that when you return to the kitchen fifteen minutes later, the bowl is empty. I'll let you in on a little secret: When it comes to food, cats are the same as dogs. They just don't let you see it.

In any event, normally when Toby and Pete get home from school, Chester comes out from wherever he's been hiding to rub up against Toby's legs and go into his little feed-me dance. This time, however, he was nowhere to be seen.

Once Howie and I had finished our afternoon snack with Toby and Pete, we set off in search of Chester.

We sniffed out his usual hiding places—under Toby's bed, on top of the computer in the den, in the laundry basket. All to no avail.

Howie even nosed Chester's favorite catnip mouse under several pieces of furniture where we wouldn't be able to fit but Chester might. Nothing.

As we trotted down the stairs after our second

search of all the bedrooms, Howie said, "Gee, Uncle Harold, maybe Pop went out the pet door while we were sleeping. Maybe he's gone after Bunnicula."

"I've already considered that," I told Howie. "The only problem is that there would be no way for him to get into the vet's office once he got there. No, I don't think that's what he—"

It was then that I heard it. Mewing. Pitiful mewing. It was coming from inside the front hall closet.

Moving quickly, I nudged the door open with my nose. There, atop a jumble of winter boots and fallen jackets, lay Chester. He looked worse than he sounded.

"Chester!" I cried out. "What's wrong?"

He responded with a deep-throated cowlike moan.

Alarmed, Howie and I went into a frenzy of barking.

Ordinarily, Chester might have told us to put a lid on it, but I noticed he wasn't complaining. I also noticed that he looked a lot like Bunnicula had been looking lately—glassy-eyed, lethargic. Maybe Mr. Monroe had been right. Maybe Bunnicula had a virus of some kind. Maybe Chester

had it now. Maybe Howie and I were next!

Just as Toby and Pete came running in from the kitchen, the front door swung open and in walked Mr. Monroe.

"What's going on?" he asked, dropping his brief-case to the floor.

"I don't know," Pete told his father. "The dogs started barking like crazy and we just got here and—"

"Look!" Toby grabbed his father's arm and pulled him toward the closet. Howie and I stopped barking as Chester, who now had all eyes upon him, filled the void with a mewling that sent chills down my spine.

"Pete, get Chester's carrier from the garage!" Mr. Monroe commanded. "We've got to get him to the doctor right away! And while we're at it . . ."

I started to slink away, but made it no farther than the bottom of the stairs before Toby had me by the collar.

". . . let's take Harold and Howie in, too, and have them checked."

I'll spare you the details of my trip to the vet. Suffice it to say it involved a lot of panting, drooling, shaking, and shedding. Fortunately, the vet knows enough to recognize normal canine behavior when he sees it, so Howie and I each received a clean bill of health and were sent home. Chester wasn't so lucky.

Of course, as I would learn later, luck had nothing to do with it. Chester was sick, all right, and he was going to have to spend the night at the vet's, but that was exactly what he wanted.

"Plant, see?" said Howie, calling out to me from inside the hall closet later that day. He had crawled in there to be close to Chester's scent and had quickly made an important discovery.

You've heard the expression "Take time to stop and smell the roses?" Well, for cats, it's "Take time to stop and eat the houseplants." So the fact that Chester had eaten Pete and Toby's Mother's Day gift to Mrs. Monroe was not altogether shocking—although he did usually exercise a little more restraint. What was surprising was the fact that he'd hidden the plant's remains in the back of the hall closet. And when I say remains, I'm talking about a few stems.

Why had he done it? It didn't take me long to figure it out.

"Plan C," I said to Howie.

"That's what I said. Plant, see?"

"No, Howie, this was Chester's Plan C. Making himself sick was his way of getting inside the animal hospital. He's gone after Bunnicula!"

"What does this mean?" Howie asked.

"It means," I said, aware that I was about to sound remarkably like Chester, "that we have a job to do, Howie."

"Oh, goody," Howie said. "Is it washing the dishes? I love that job. Although the last time I licked all the plates clean, Mrs. Monroe came into the kitchen and got all upset as if I'd left some food on them or something. Which I happen to know for a fact I did not. So this time—"

"Howie!" I snapped. Now I *really* felt like Chester. "Not that kind of job. A mission, a duty! We have to catch up with Chester before it's too late!"

"Then let's go!" Howie yipped enthusiastically. "We can wash the dishes later!"

Luckily, the Monroes had gone out for the evening, so it was easy to let ourselves out the pet door and be on our way. And although I hadn't thought so earlier, it was also a piece of luck that we'd been to the vet's that day and I had paid attention, because now I knew how to get there. The only problem was how we were going to break in. And then a third piece of luck fell into place. Howie said something that gave me the answer.

"Wait a minute, Uncle Harold," he said, coming to a sudden halt after we'd been walking for a few minutes. "We're not going back to where that skunk was, are we?"

"No," I said. "That was Upper Centerville. We're going in the opposite direction."

"Good, because that skunk makes me think

about counterfeit pennies, you know why?"

"Why?"

"Bad scents. Get it, Uncle Harold? Huh, do you get it?"

I chuckled indulgently. "Yes, Howie," I said, "very funny."

Encouraged, Howie went on. "Do you know what the judge said when the skunk walked in? Odor in the court! Odor in the court! Hey, Uncle Harold, what did one skunk say to the other skunk when he bowed his head? Let us spray! I got a million of 'em, Uncle Harold."

"Well, save some for a rainy day," I told Howie, but he went on anyway. I wasn't listening, however, because his mentioning the skunk had brought to my mind Bob and Linda. And thinking of Bob and Linda gave me the answer to my problem.

EIGHT

Friends and Traitors

"WHAT are we doing *here?*" Howie asked a short time later. "I thought you said we were going to the vet's, but here we are at the movies. Can I get some popcorn?"

"I'm afraid we're not going to the movies—or the movie theater," I explained to Howie. "We're looking for—"

I stopped myself when I spotted them coming around the corner of the alley they called their office. There was no mistaking that scrawny gray cat and her fat tabby sidekick. It was Felony and Miss Demeanor, all right. Sisters in crime. Cat burglars. If anyone would know how to break into a locked building, those two would.

"Felony!" I called out. "Miss Demeanor!"

They stopped in their tracks, Miss Demeanor clumsily stumbling into Felony's backside, nearly toppling her over. Felony turned and snarled at her companion, who responded with, "Oh yeah, you and who else?" Ah, they'd lost none of their charm!

Felony looked in my direction. "Who wants us?" she called out in a voice she probably picked up from watching old gangster movies on cable.

Howie ran to them, yipping happily. "It's us, it's us! Howie and Harold! Remember? From Chateau Bow-Wow last summer?"

As I loped along behind Howie, I could see Felony's eyes giving us the once-over. When she did it again, I wanted to ask if it was now called a twice-over but thought better of it.

Suddenly, recognition lit up her eyes as if someone had turned on a switch.

"Hey, Miss D.," she shouted over her shoulder.

Miss Demeanor, who was maybe an inch behind her, shouted back, "What?"

"It's two of those three bozos we met at Chateau Bow-Wow."

Miss Demeanor, who looked like she'd have to be completely rewired before anything lit up her blank eyes, drawled, "Uh-huh."

Felony scowled. "We ain't got all night, Miss D. Let me give ya a little hint: Cute Whiskers."

"Ooooo," the fat tabby purred. Cute Whiskers is what she had called Chester. "Now I remember. So where is he?" She looked on either side of us as if we might be hiding him somewhere.

"That's why we came to see you," I said. "You see, Chester is missing."

"I always said he was missing," Felony quipped. "Missing half a deck!" She chortled merrily and Miss Demeanor joined in.

"No, no, I mean he's really missing," I persevered. I explained that it was imperative we break into the animal hospital and rescue Chester right away. I didn't go into too many details. I was afraid they'd end up siding with Chester and want to help him instead of me. Besides, I had the feeling Felony and Miss Demeanor weren't exactly cut out for handling more than a few details at a time.

"I dunno," Felony said when I'd finished. "We

wuz on our way to a big caper. We haven't got a lotta time to spare."

"It won't take much time," I promised. "All you have to do is find a way in. We'll take it from there."

Felony turned up a corner of her mouth and made a strange sucking sound. I gathered this was an outward manifestation of some deep inner mental activity.

"Well *(slurp, snap, suck)*, I guess *(snap, slurp, pop)* we could consider it *(slurp, suck, sizzle)* . . ."

In desperation, I turned to Miss Demeanor. "Don't do it for us," I pleaded. "Do it for Cute Whiskers."

I couldn't believe I actually referred to Chester as Cute Whiskers. The words curdled in my mouth. But they worked.

"Yer right, Harold," said Miss Demeanor. "Come on, Felony, we gotta help out our fella feline. After all, he helped us out once."

"Yeah, yeah, yeah *(smack, slurp, smack)*." Felony lowered the corner of her mouth, then turned her head in either direction to make sure she wasn't being overheard. "We're breakin' into the Big Belly

Deli, see, and we gotta time it just right. We can't be late, got it?"

"I got it," I said. "Then you'll do it?"

"Yeah, we'll do it—seein' as how it's fer Chester an' all."

As we walked away, Miss Demeanor began to purr loudly. "We're gonna sneak inta the Big Belly Deli at closin' time and party all night," she said. "I'm havin' a corned beef and sardine on rye, and that's just fer starters."

"And I'm havin' bologna and herring on pumpernickel," said Felony, "with mustard and maybe a little Tabasco sauce. And then I'm havin' . . ."

By the time we reached the animal hospital, I wasn't sure if I was starved or never wanted to eat again.

It was just starting to get dark. Luckily, there were very few people around, so it was easy to check out the premises without being noticed. The problem was, the premises appeared to be sealed tight.

Staring at the heavily bolted back entrance to the building, I sighed. "What was I thinking? There's no way we can get in."

Felony cleared her throat. "I did not come all

this way to be insulted," she said. "You are dealing with professionals here, Harold. If you thought this was going to be a piece of cake, would you have called in professionals?"

"Oh, yeah," said Miss Demeanor, "and that reminds me—and then I'm gonna have a piece of marble pound cake with a side of potato salad."

"Did you ever read *The Potato Has a Thousand Eyes*?" Howie asked.

Miss Demeanor's eyes took on the dull luster of tarnished brass. "Read?" she said.

I sensed we were getting a wee bit off course.

"Felony," I said, "how do you imagine—"

"Window!" Felony snapped.

"But—"

"I was thinkin' we'd have to go in through the ducts, but looky there, Harold."

I raised my head in the direction Felony indicated. There, not two feet above my head, was a window. It was open only a crack, but if the two cat burglars could jimmy it all the way, the opening would be large enough for both Howie and me to fit through easily.

"That's lucky," I said.

Felony turned to Miss D. "Crowbar," she said.

"Crowbar," Miss D. repeated.

Within minutes, the two cats had come up with a makeshift crowbar and had the window halfway open. I had to admire their dexterity and skill.

From the other side of the window, I heard a familiar voice call out, "Who is it? Who's there?"

"Oh, yoo-hoo, hunky boy!" Miss Demeanor called out. I cringed on Chester's behalf. "We're comin' to get ya, Cute Whiskers!"

"Cute Whiskers?" I heard Chester repeat from inside. "Is it . . . is that . . . ?"

"One, two, three!" Felony commanded. The two cats arched their backs against the half-open window and forced it all the way up. We were home-free.

"It is I! It is me! It is we! It is us!" cried Miss Demeanor in a bravado display of grammatical insecurity.

I too became insecure at that moment, worrying that the two cats would jump inside and free Chester before I could stop them. I was saved by a remarkable stroke of luck.

A clock tower chimed eight times.

"It's closin' time at the Big Belly Deli!" Felony shrieked. "We're gonna be late!"

"Aw, can't I just say hello to Cute Whiskers?" Miss Demeanor whined.

"Pastrami and lox on an onion roll!" was Felony's reply.

Miss Demeanor jumped down from the windowsill. "Gotta run," she said. "Say hi to Cute Whiskers for me, will ya, Harold?"

"Thank . . ." I said to the two cats as they streaked off into the night, ". . . you."

"Harold, Harold? Is that you?" Chester called out. "What's going on out there?"

With the help of a garbage pail, I leaped up onto the windowsill, then lifted Howie up by the nape of his neck. The two of us dropped down into the dimly lit back room of the veterinarian's office. I felt like a hero in a war movie.

As my eyes adjusted to the light, I saw Chester staring down at us from a nearby cage.

"Chester!" I cried. "How are you feeling?"

"Greenbriar gave me some kind of medicine that made me sleep most of the day. Right now, my mouth feels like somebody lined it with mouse fur, but other than that I'm feeling a lot better. You've got to get me out of here, Harold!"

It suddenly occurred to me how quiet the place was.

"Where is everybody?" I asked.

"I'm the only one here."

"But where's Bunnicula?" Howie inquired.

"He's gone."

Howie began to whimper. "Gone? To the big carrot patch in the sky? The bunny beyond? The hareafter? The hoppy hunting ground? The—"

"He escaped!" Chester exploded.

"Oh," said Howie.

"That's why you've got to get me out of here! I've got to stop him before it's too late."

"Was this his cage?" Howie asked. He was looking in at a ground-level cage next to him.

"As a matter of fact, yes," said Chester. "Why do you ask?"

"Look, Uncle Harold," said Howie. "Look at the newspaper lining the bottom."

I looked. It was Saturday's paper. There was a big ad in the middle of the page:

CENTERVILLE CINEMA—THE LAST PICTURE SHOW!

**SEE THE MOVIE THAT OPENED
THIS LANDMARK THEATER IN 1931!**

DRACULA, STARRING BELA LUGOSI

TRANSYLVANIA COMES TO CENTERVILLE!

BE THERE . . . IF YOU DARE!!

If Bunnicula hadn't thought before of looking for his mother at the movie theater, there was no question in my mind now that that is where he had gone. I knew what I had to do.

And I knew what I couldn't do.

"Come on, Harold, get me out of here. It can't be that hard to unlock this cage. I'll talk you through it."

I looked up at my friend, my best friend, my oldest friend in the world, and I said, "I'm afraid I can't do that, Chester."

"Oh, now, Harold," Chester said, "of course you can. I'm sorry for all the times I've called you a dunce or a simpleton—"

"Or a dolt," I said.

"Or a dolt," Chester went on, "but I know you're not really *that* dumb. I'm sure you can figure out how to open the door and get me out of here."

"It's not that I can't do it, Chester," I said. "It's that I *won't* do it."

I looked away, but I could hear in the silence that Chester understood what I was saying.

"I thought you were my friend," he said at last.

My heart lay heavy in my chest. "I am your friend, but I'm Bunnicula's friend, too, and I can't let you hurt him. I've stood by you in all your crazy attempts to do him in in the past, but I . . . Well, I just can't do it anymore, Chester. I'm sorry."

Chester's voice was like a shard of ice that cut through me. "Sorry?" he said. "That's what you have to say after all the years we've been friends? Sorry? Well, here's what I'm sorry about, Harold. I'm sorry that I can't be your friend anymore."

I looked up. "Chester," I said.

But he turned his back on me and said nothing. Nothing, that is, but one word, which he spat out at me as Howie and I made our way back out through the open window.

"Traitor," he said.

When Howie and I emerged into the outside world, the air felt different. Where it had been warm and springlike before, now all I felt was a chill. All I wanted was for everything to be the way it once had been. And all I knew was that it never would be. I had lost my best friend. How I ached to go home and curl up in a dark corner where I could sleep for days. But I couldn't go home. I had to find Bunnicula. How was he to know that the newspaper in his cage was from two days earlier? There would be no movie shown tonight, just an empty, dangerous theater perilously close to being destroyed.

As we set off to find Bunnicula, Chester's final word repeated itself over and over in my mind.

Traitor. Traitor. Traitor.

NINE

The Last Showdown

BY the time Howie and I reached the movie theater, the night sky was not only chilly but dark. I could make out several large trucks parked out front, one of which held a tall crane with an ominous steel ball hanging from the end of it, and everywhere there were police barricades and banners bearing the words DEMOLITION SITE, DO NOT CROSS. All I could think was that somewhere inside that darkened, haunted-looking theater was a weak and sickly bunny searching for his mother. Was she even in there? Or was Bunnicula pursuing a memory, a wish, a phantom?

"Are w-we g-g-going in there?" Howie stammered next to me. "It looks scary, Uncle Harold. Like *Night of the Living Gargoyles.*"

"Excuse me?"

"Number eighteen. There's this boy, see . . ."

"Howie," I said, "we have to get Bunnicula out of there before the building is torn down tomorrow."

"What about his mother?"

"Yes, well, we'll get her out, too, of course." I didn't tell Howie that I had serious doubts Bunnicula's mother was in there.

I also had serious doubts we would be in there anytime soon. This was a challenge that would have stumped Felony and Miss Demeanor. It was too dark to find a way in—and even if we did get past all the barricades and doors locked with chains, it would probably be pitch-black. Besides, I told myself, if we looked for Bunnicula now, the Monroes would miss us. No, it would be better to return first thing in the morning, when there was light.

Howie didn't give me an argument. He was as glad as I was to be out of there. And the Monroes were glad to see us when we returned.

Howie, being young and without worries, slept soundly that night. I did not. When I wasn't worrying about whether we'd be able to rescue Bunnicula before the wrecking crew did its work, I was thinking about what had happened between Chester and me. I kept thinking how only days before I had been so happy that things were normal around our house and how quickly everything had changed. Not everything, perhaps, but the friendship that mattered most to me in the world had been destroyed. And by my own doing. Had I been right to do it? I couldn't let Chester harm Bunnicula. I had to draw the line somewhere. So why was it that every time I licked my lips that night I tasted salt?

Just before dawn I fell asleep, only to be awakened a short time later by Toby's cry of "Do I *have* to go?"

"No," I heard Mrs. Monroe say, "you don't have to go. You can go over to Jared's house if you want."

"You're such a wuss," Pete said to his brother. "Don't you want to see it get knocked down? It's going to be *so* cool!"

"If you're going to cheer," Mrs. Monroe said then, "maybe you should go to Kyle's house, Pete. Our committee is going to register one final protest. No, it won't stop the wrecking ball at this point, but it's important for us to be there as a voice, as a conscience, Pete. The movie house is the most beautiful and architecturally interesting building in

Centerville. It should be preserved, not torn down. We live in a throwaway society. Someone has to be there to say, 'This is wrong.' Do you understand?"

"Can I have chocolate milk for breakfast?" Pete asked.

Mrs. Monroe sighed. "It's 'may I,' and yes, you may," she said.

"I want to be a conscience," Toby piped up. "Like you and Dad. I'll go."

Conscience. There was something about that word—and then my fuzzy, half-awake brain remembered.

"Howie!" I cried.

Howie jumped up from where he was sleeping and bumped his head on the underside of the coffee table.

"Ouch! What?" he asked.

I answered with one word: "Bunnicula!"

We were out of the house in ten minutes flat. Okay, we might have been faster if we hadn't stopped off in the kitchen to have breakfast first. But we needed our strength. Besides, we didn't want to make the Monroes suspicious.

By the time we got to the theater, a crowd was already beginning to gather. There were even a couple of reporters and TV cameras. And there, standing near the trucks, were several burly men glancing at their watches.

"They're going to start tearing the building down soon," I said to Howie. "I hope we didn't wait too long!"

Making sure we weren't being watched, we sneaked down the alley next to the theater until we came to a door marked STAGE ENTRANCE. Luckily, it was open, probably to allow the workers to make their final preparations.

"Okay, Howie, this is it," I said. "We've got to move fast. Are you nervous?"

"Wh-h-h-h-ho, m-m-m-m-me?" Howie replied. His tongue was hanging out of his mouth, his breath was coming in quick, short pants. "N-n-n-no, I'm n-n-not n-n-n-n-nervous!"

I decided this was no time for a debate. "Good," I said, "then let's go."

The theater was dark and cool inside. Enough light leaked through from cracks and windows here and there to help us see where we were going, but we still managed to bump into things with every fifth or sixth step. Every time we did, Howie would yip excitedly.

"Ssh!" I admonished him. "We don't want to scare Bunnicula."

And then softly, softly I called out his name: "Bun-nic-ula! Bun-nic-ula!"

"Bunnicula!" Howie echoed. "It's us, Howie and Harold."

The farther we crept into the abandoned theater, the creepier the shadows became, the eerier the silence. At one point, I thought I heard something moving. I stopped and listened and realized that all I'd been hearing was the pounding of my own heart.

We were in the middle of a very large and very empty room. Having never been in a movie theater before, I couldn't make much sense of it. Then I remembered Mr. Monroe saying that all the seats were being taken out before the demolition began. Apparently, this was the room where people came to watch the movies. There at one end was a big white wall. And there at the other end was a wall with two doors in it. Very high in the center of that wall was a small square opening neatly framing the silhouette of a figure—a figure with two tall ears.

"Bunnicula," I said in a hushed voice.

Howie heard me and looked up, too.

"But, Uncle Harold," he said, "How can Bunnicula be awake? It's daytime."

"There's no sunlight in here," I pointed out. "Bunnicula must think it's still night. Now come on—we don't have a moment to lose."

As we made our way cautiously out of the large, empty room, through one of the doors, and up a set of stairs that would take us—I hoped—to the small square opening in the wall that held our friend Bunnicula, I heard the same clock I'd heard the night before. Only now, it chimed nine times.

Nine o'clock. Why, I asked myself, did that seem significant?

And then I remembered. The demolition was scheduled to begin at nine o'clock this Tuesday morning.

I picked up the pace, and Howie scampered after me. At the top of the stairs, we came to a half-open door. Behind it was a small room—and there on the wall to our left was the opening we'd seen from below. In the shadowy light, I could make out a pair of eyes glistening. Red eyes. Frightened eyes.

"Bunnicula!" I cried.

I was all set to leap up and grab him by the neck

when another set of eyes stopped me dead in my tracks.

"Uncle Harold!" Howie called out in alarm. He too had seen them. I could hear him panting rapidly behind me.

"Is it B-Bunnicula's m-mother?" he sputtered.

Was it? I asked myself. Or was it someone else? Some*thing* else? Had Howie's FleshCrawler books gotten to me? Was I imagining some sort of creature who lived in the movie theater, some beast who was about to leap out from the shadows and attack?

There was no time to waste. Either the beast would get us or the wrecking ball would.

"Who are you?" I demanded. "What do you want?"

"Oh, I think you know who I am," a familiar voice said. "And I know you know what I want."

"Chester!" I cried. "But how—"

"How did I get here?" Chester said, stepping out into a pale pool of light. His eyes looked unnatural, possessed. "Oh, it was easy enough, thanks to last night's handiwork of a couple of criminal kitties. When Greenbriar opened my cage this morning, I made a dash for it before he spotted the open window. I got here moments before you did, Harold. Oh, and by the way, whatever you had planned, forget it. Bunnicula is mine!"

"But what are you going to do?"

Chester bounded up to the opening in the wall with a single leap. Bunnicula barely budged. I could tell the poor thing was terrified.

"What am I going to do? I'll tell you what I'm going to do," Chester said.

But that was all he had time to say, for suddenly there was a thunderous roar, and before we knew what was happening, the wall to our right exploded.

"Run!" I heard Chester cry.

I looked up at the opening in the wall and to my horror watched as Chester and Bunnicula, locked in a deadly embrace, tumbled from the precipice. The scene from the story Toby had read to me flooded my mind, its words, its images exploding within me even as the room seemed to be exploding around me. I thought of Chester, my dear friend, who had so recently called me traitor, and the words of the story came back to me: "It was the last that I was ever destined to see of him in this world."

Before the terrible wrecking ball could strike again, I ordered Howie to run for his life. I ran, too. And I didn't look back.

TEN

One of the Family

"HAROLD!" Toby cried out. "Howie!"

Frantically, I raced toward my young master even as I searched the onrushing crowd for signs of Chester and Bunnicula, hoping against hope that they had miraculously escaped and were somehow already out there in front of the theater. But as Toby threw his arms around me, I knew that the only ones to have escaped were Howie and me.

"Are you okay, boy?" Toby asked. "What are you doing here?"

Mrs. Monroe had picked Howie up and was trying to comfort him, but Howie was squirming to be free.

"We've got to go back, Uncle Harold!" he yipped. "We've got to rescue Pop and Bunnicula!"

Mrs. Monroe seemed to understand. Perhaps people were more intelligent than Chester and I had been willing to give them credit for.

"Stop the demolition!" she cried out. "There may be other animals inside!"

"Stop the demolition!" someone echoed.

The trucks and the noise came to a sudden halt.

Breaking free of Toby's embrace, I charged down the alleyway to the back of the theater. Howie, who must have leaped from Mrs. Monroe's arms at the same time, was fast on my heels. Barking for everything we were worth, we led an impromptu rescue team, complete with flashlights and TV news cameras, into the partially decimated movie house.

"Be careful!" someone warned.

"Just follow the dogs," another voice called out. "They seem to know what they're doing."

A fine thing, I thought. Does that mean most of the time we *don't* seem to know what we're doing? I didn't dwell on the thought, however. I had more important matters to attend to. Matters of life and death.

There must have been a second blow of the

wrecking ball as Howie and I had been fleeing the building, because the wall that had held the small square hole where we'd first spotted Bunnicula and from which he and Chester had tumbled was gone. In its place was a large pile of rubble.

I stared at the pile with a sick, sinking feeling in my stomach.

"Chester!" I woofed.

At first there was no response. But then I heard it. The same sort of pitiful mew I'd heard coming from the closet only—was it possible?—the day before. This time it was not a sickly mew, but a frightened one.

"There!" I heard Mr. Monroe call out. "Let me have that flashlight!"

A beam of light bounced off the walls and floor and fallen pieces of plaster and concrete and wood, and then suddenly it caught something. Something alive! It was Chester, wide-eyed and panting!

Howie and I bounded across the room. "Chester!" I cried. "You're all right!"

He didn't respond, but just kept staring at all of us.

"What about . . . What about Bunnicula?" Howie asked.

Chester did the strangest thing then. He howled. Or so it seemed. He lifted his head high and let out the most piercing cry. Was he hurt?

"Chester, it's all right, boy!" Mr. Monroe said, brushing against me as he extended a hand to Chester. "Come here, boy," snapping his fingers. "Come on, it's all right, Chester. Everything will be fine."

But Chester didn't go to Mr. Monroe. On the contrary, the closer Mr. Monroe got, the more Chester hissed and spat.

"Maybe he's been injured," another man said.

"He might be in shock," said Mrs. Monroe. "That's possible, isn't it?"

I felt Toby's hand stroke my head. "Is he going to be all right?" he asked his parents. "Is Chester going to be all right?"

A big man who looked like he might have been a member of the wrecking crew worked his way through the small crowd that had followed us inside. "I'll take care of this," he said brusquely.

He walked up to Chester and started to grab him. "Come on, kitty," he said, "you're coming with me now."

He didn't know who he was messing with. Chester swiped him with his claws.

"*Yeeouch!*" the man said. "Hey, what gives?"

Chester turned to me. "Help me, Harold," he said. "You're my friend, aren't you?"

"I never stopped being your friend," I said.

"Then help me save Bunnicula."

"*Save* Bunnicula?" I repeated.

"You heard me," Chester said.

And then I understood. Bunnicula was somewhere in the pile of rubble Chester was sitting on. And Chester wasn't moving until Bunnicula had been found.

"Come on, Howie," I said, "we have one more job to do. A dog's job."

We moved toward the pile of rubble and sniffed. It didn't take long to catch Bunnicula's scent. Once we had it, we began to bark.

"The dogs are trying to tell us something," a woman said. "There's something else in there." Turning to the Monroes, she asked, "Do you have any other pets?"

"A rabbit," said Mr. Monroe, "but why would *he* be here?"

"There's something strange going on, Robert," Mrs. Monroe said to her husband, and then she said to the others, "Our vet called us this morning to tell us Bunnicula—that's our rabbit—wasn't in his cage when he arrived this morning. And soon after that Chester escaped."

"Well," said the big man Chester had lashed out at a few minutes earlier, "it looks to me like there may just be a rabbit in that rubble."

All at once, everyone began to dig.

"I see eyes!" someone called out. "Red eyes!"

"Bunnicula!" Pete shouted when the bunny came into view at last. "This is so crazy! What are the animals doing here?"

I don't know if the Monroes ever got that question answered to their satisfaction. I don't know if they really cared. All that mattered was that we were all safe and sound—even Bunnicula, who had miraculously survived because of a large beam that had fallen in such a way as to create a little cave in the debris where he had hidden. He didn't appear to have even a scratch. But you could see that his little heart was beating rapidly—and those red eyes had never looked more terrified.

The only thing predictable about Chester is his unpredictability, and in the next moment he did the most unpredictable thing I'd ever seen. He jumped down—and began to lick Bunnicula!

"What are you doing?" I cried.

"For heaven's sake, Harold," he said. "Use your brain, such as it is. I'm letting him know it's all right. Can't you see how scared he is?"

There was a flash of light as a camera recorded the moment. And *that* was the image that made the evening news and the next day's front page in the *Courier:*

CAT SAVES RABBIT—THE LAST SHOW

AT THE CENTERVILLE CINEMA

For the record, Howie and I were given some credit, too, but it was the picture of Chester wrapped around the terrified Bunnicula, licking him, that got the most attention. I had to chuckle to think that Chester had earned his brief moment of fame because of his kindness to a rabbit. And not just any rabbit—his archenemy, the vampire rabbit Bunnicula!

*   *   *

It was some time before things returned to what passes for normal at the Monroe house. Our odd behavior, strange disappearances, and reappearances in unexpected places took some sorting out, and to this day I don't think the Monroes have all the answers. Truth be told, I'm not sure we do, either. I think we were right about Bunnicula's missing his mother, although of course he never said a thing. That was why he had run to the theater when he saw the ad in the newspaper. But was she really "out there" somewhere as Chester suggested? I doubt it. I suspect once she had left her baby bunny at that theater years earlier, she had gone on her way, trusting in the kindness of strangers and hoping for the best.

Now the theater itself no longer exists, and so

for Bunnicula there truly is no going home again. But then, that movie theater was no more his home than Chateau Bow-Wow was Howie's or the animal shelter where the Monroes had found me as a puppy was mine. Chester, who as a kitten was given to Mr. Monroe as a birthday present, has no memory of where he came from. But it doesn't really matter. When you're a pet, your home is with your people and your people are your family.

The reason Bunnicula missed his mother, I think, was that he never felt entirely at home here—not as long as Chester was threatening his very existence. But that's all changed.

"So you're no longer worried that Bunnicula is a vampire, eh, Chester?" I said one evening after dinner. Howie, Chester, and I were sprawled out on the front porch enjoying the warm spring breezes.

"Nonsense, Harold," Chester replied snappishly. "Of course he's a vampire."

"Then why are you no longer trying to do him in?"

Chester yawned elaborately, letting me know that the topic of conversation was barely worth the bother. "Really, Harold," he said, "it's so obvious.

Vampires are indestructible. Don't you see? When Bunnicula wasn't killed in that pile of rubble at the movie theater, I suddenly came to understand that he had powers beyond defeat. How would I ever overcome such powers and save an unsuspecting world?"

"How, indeed?" I asked, bemused.

"No, no, I figured it was best to return Bunnicula to where he rightfully belongs. Who knows him like I do, Harold? Who better to use that knowledge in a different way than I have used it in the past to keep a close eye on him and make sure he does no harm?"

"So you've become his guardian, is that it, Chester? His protector?"

"In a way. Though I think of myself more as protecting him from himself."

I smiled and said nothing. I think I understood then that Chester had never really meant to destroy Bunnicula. He may have wanted to destroy the evil he thought Bunnicula represented, but Bunnicula himself? He was just a bunny. More than that, he was one of the family.

Now Chester has taken to napping next to Bunnicula's cage. The two of them sometimes sleep so that their backs touch and, although I would never embarrass him by pointing it out, I've noticed that Chester purrs loudest at those times. And Bunnicula? The sparkle is back is in his eyes and the bounce is back in his step.

If there was any doubt that a new relationship had been forged between Chester and his Moriarty, however, it was answered one morning when I crept downstairs to sing Bunnicula to sleep. Imagine my surprise when I heard a familiar voice singing those familiar words in my stead. I stopped and listened. It was surprising enough that Chester knew the lullaby, but my astonishment was even greater when at the song's end, I heard hard-hearted old Chester utter the words: "Sweet dreams, Bunnicula, old pal."

As for Chester and me, we're back to being the best of friends. Chester understood that I was only trying to do what I thought was best for Bunnicula. And I understood that Chester was just being himself.

Howie, having lived through his own scary adventure, no longer reads FleshCrawlers. He says they're not realistic enough for him. But they did inspire him to begin writing stories of his own. He asked me to look at them, which I did, and I've told him he's pretty good—for a puppy. He still has a lot to learn, of course.

"Will you teach me, Uncle Harold?" he asked me the last time I read one of his stories. I told him I would. Who knows? Maybe he'll write books one day just as I have. Anything is possible.